TRANSFORMERS ENERGON BRAND™

OFFICIAL GUIDEBOOK

written by Michael Teitelbaum

CONTENTS

Reader's Digest Children's Books™

Pleasantville, New York • Montréal, Québec • Bath, United Kingdom

ENERGON

ENERGON IN
ITS RAW FORM

Energon is the most powerful source of energy ever discovered. It boosts the power of Transformers to mind-shattering levels and it can also provide a clean source of energy for humans on Earth. Whoever controls Energon, controls the universe. Because of this, the evil Decepticons will stop at nothing to grab all the Energon in the universe and use its power to crush their enemies, the Autobots.

The Decepticons send Terrorcons, who attack like swarms of deadly insects, to steal Energon from Earth. The Terrorcons suck the powerful energy out of rocks or asteroids. Then they bring the Energon back to Unicron, a planet-sized Transformer, and drop it into his dark, cavernous mouth. (See page 4.)

But this powerful energy source is unpredictable and dangerous. It must be refined before it is safe to use. The Autobots use Transformers called Omnicons to refine Energon. The Omnicons take the raw Energon and create Energon chips. However, the extra Energon power only lasts for a short time. When the chips stop glowing, the energy is gone.

The discovery of Energon on Earth has once again made the planet a battlefield in the Transformers' ongoing war.

ENERGON IN ITS REFINED FORM

UNICRON

PROFILE

Unicron is the largest Transformer that ever existed. He is neither Autobot nor Decepticon. Unicron is the size of a planet and he feeds off the destruction of other planets, pulling their energy into his enormous body.

This planet-eating robot was greatly damaged during the Unicron Battles. The damage to Unicron was so extensive that only vast amounts of Energon can restore his former power.

As the Transformers Energon saga begins to unfold, Megatron, leader of the Decepticons, is trapped inside Unicron. He has become entangled in Unicron's Spark Chamber, the control center of the giant robot. Gaining control of the leaderless Decepticons, Unicron sends the Decepticons, along with the deadly Terrorcons, to bring him all of the Energon on Earth. Unicron's goal is to suck the planet dry of the valuable energy source. When he has captured all of Earth's Energon, Unicron will once again be the most powerful force in the universe.

UNICRON IN PLANET FORM

PROFILE

A period of relative peace followed the destructive battles between the Autobots and Decepticons over the Mini-cons. During that time, the Autobots established cities all over the universe.

On Earth, the Autobots set up an undersea city. Most of the time, this city rests on the ocean floor. It can, however, be raised up to float on the surface of the water. When the city is raised to the ocean's surface, a long bridge extends and connects it to land. Other Autobot cities on earth are located in Mexico, England, and Egypt.

An Autobot research center exists on Cybertron, the Transformers' home planet. Here, parts for Transformers and battle armor worn by humans are made. Another Autobot city can be found in the asteroid belt in Earth's solar system. Long, clear tubes connect the asteroids to each other, forming the huge city. It was here that Energon was first discovered.

The Autobot city on Mars was the first of the Autobot cities to be attacked by Terrorcons. They were sent by Unicron to steal the Energon from Mars. The Autobot city on Earth's moon is located deep inside a crater. Much Energon has been excavated from the moon, making it a prime target for the Terrorcons.

OPTIMUS PRIME

POWER SCALE

RANK	10.0	ENDURANCE	10.0
STRENGTH	10.0	COURAGE	10.0
INTELLIGENCE	10.0	FIREBLAST	10.0
SPEED	10.0	SKILL	10.0

QUOTE: "THOSE WHO THREATEN PEACE WILL FALL IN PIECES."

PROFILE

Optimus Prime is the wise and powerful leader of the Autobots. He possesses incredible strength, great courage, and is a skillful warrior and commander. He believes strongly that freedom is the right of all living beings and he will fight fiercely to protect that freedom. A peaceful solution is always his first choice. But Optimus Prime will not hesitate to use his tremendous power and arsenal of weapons. He must stop the Decepticons and Terrorcons from stealing Earth's vast supply of Energon. He is determined to prevent Unicron from regaining power and bringing his unspeakable evil to the universe.

OPTIMUS PRIME IN VEHICLE FORM

FACT FILE

- Optimus Prime trains a team of young Autobots on Cybertron, including Ironhide. In time, they will take their place beside the Autobots' leader.

- Optimus Prime teaches his young Prime Squad the "Kumite," a system of ancient Autobot combat techniques.

SUPER OPTIMUS PRIME

POWER SCALE

RANK	10.0	ENDURANCE	10.0
STRENGTH	10.0	COURAGE	10.0
INTELLIGENCE	10.0	FIREBLAST	10.0
SPEED	10.0	SKILL	10.0

QUOTE: "FREEDOM IS THE RIGHT OF
ALL SENTIENT BEINGS."

PROFILE

When Optimus Prime discovered that Unicron was gaining power and seeking large sources of Energon, he knew that both Earth and Cybertron were in danger. He returned to Cybertron and, in a special ceremony, received the Spark of Combination from the all-powerful Primus, source of all Autobot power. The Spark of Combination allows Transformers to link together and combine into more powerful forms. Using the power of the Spark of Combination, Optimus Prime becomes Super Optimus Prime, his most powerful form. In this form, he combines his tractor-trailer vehicle form with four other vehicles—a fire truck, a helicopter, a submersible underwater vehicle, and a drilling vehicle.

SUPER OPTIMUS PRIME
AND HIS TEAM
IN VEHICLE FORM

FACT FILE

- Super Optimus Prime's tractor-trailer acts as an Energon-filled tower when he's in his vehicle mode.

- To join Optimus Prime's elite Prime Squad, a Transformer must be officially granted the Spark of Combination.

HOT SHOT

POWER SCALE

RANK	8.0	ENDURANCE	8.0
STRENGTH	7.0	COURAGE	9.0
INTELLIGENCE	8.0	FIREBLAST	7.0
SPEED	10.0	SKILL	9.0

QUOTE: "THERE IS NO GREATER TEACHER
THAN EXPERIENCE!"

PROFILE

Once a young, stubborn, impatient warrior, Hot Shot has grown up. He is now a seasoned veteran of combat. His gutsy, skillful, courageous performance during the Unicron battles proved to Optimus Prime that he had become a skilled fighter with great leadership abilities. Experience and wisdom have replaced his headstrong desire to rush into battle before thinking. His outstanding knowledge of combat tactics and his strategic thinking ability have made him a top-notch soldier. Hot Shot is one of the fastest Autobots, whether in his robot mode or in his vehicle mode of a speedy sports car.

POWERLINX HOTSHOT

HOT SHOT IN VEHICLE FORM

FACT FILE

- When Hot Shot changes into his vehicle mode, he becomes a powerful sports car, possessing even greater speed.

- Hot Shot has two powerful weapons – his amazing speed and a powerful blaster weapon attached to his body.

INFERNO

POWER SCALE

RANK	8.0	ENDURANCE	10.0
STRENGTH	8.0	COURAGE	10.0
INTELLIGENCE	7.0	FIREBLAST	10.0
SPEED	8.0	SKILL	10.0

QUOTE: "ALWAYS LOOK BEFORE YOU LEAP."

PROFILE

Inferno is a first-class Autobot warrior. His main concern during battle is always the safety and well-being of those around him. In his robot mode, he is quiet and mild-mannered, with a positive outlook. He is also a skilled marksman capable of great stealth. A deeply principled Autobot, he takes his commitment to others and to freedom very seriously. In his vehicle mode, he is a powerful, heroic fire truck, willing to take on dangerous search-and-rescue missions. Inferno always thinks before he acts. He is known for coming up with well-conceived battle plans, knowing that his actions have important consequences.

INFERNO IN VEHICLE FORM

POWERLINX INFERNO

FACT FILE

- Inferno can use the Spark of Combination to powerlink with Hot Shot, creating a fast, powerful, and clever combination Transformer.

- Inferno is an expert on technical systems, tools, and targeted weapons such as Energon missiles.

IRONHIDE

PROFILE

Ironhide is a young and eager Autobot recruit. He is a strong fighter, but is often reckless and undisciplined. He believes he is ready to join Optimus Prime's elite Prime Squad, but the Autobot leader feels that Ironhide is not yet mature enough. Ironhide also hopes to powerlink with Optimus Prime, but again he will have to wait. Still, he is a fierce fighter. His powerful laser cannon is greatly feared by the Decepticons. In time, Ironhide should develop into a seasoned and disciplined warrior.

IRONHIDE IN VEHICLE FORM

POWERLINX IRONHIDE

POWER SCALE

RANK	5.0	ENDURANCE	8.0
STRENGTH	9.0	COURAGE	8.0
INTELLIGENCE	7.0	FIREBLAST	8.0
SPEED	6.0	SKILL	7.0

QUOTE: "IF TROUBLE DOESN'T FIND ME, I'LL FIND IT."

FACT FILE

- Ironhide can powerlink with Jetfire, greatly increasing their combined strength to a mighty, Decepticon-crushing level.

JETFIRE

PROFILE

Jetfire is a skilled and seasoned Autobot warrior. He is one of Optimus Prime's oldest and most trusted friends, and they have fought side by side in many battles. He projects a carefree personality among his Autobot teammates to keep things loose. But when the battle begins, he is a serious warrior. Jetfire prides himself on being an excellent teacher in the ways of combat. He has committed himself to training Ironhide, vowing to develop the young Transformer into a battle-ready fighter.

JETFIRE IN VEHICLE FORM

POWER SCALE

RANK	10.0	ENDURANCE	8.0
STRENGTH	8.0	COURAGE	9.0
INTELLIGENCE	7.0	FIREBLAST	9.0
SPEED	10.0	SKILL	8.0

QUOTE: "EAT MY VAPOR TRAIL!"

FACT FILE

- Jetfire can powerlink with his young pupil, Ironhide. The two grow very strong in their combined form, as Jetfire trains Ironhide in the ways of the warrior.

POWERLINX JETFIRE

RODIMUS

PROFILE

Rodimus is a young, rebellious warrior. He is a foreman of the Omnicons. He splits his time between making sure that Energon is processed on time and rushing headlong into battle. He is wild, headstrong, aggressive, and he loves danger. He will often act before thinking. In his vehicle mode of a racing semitruck, Rodimus can reach amazing speeds. In his robot mode, he uses a powerful Energon cannon in combat with the Decepticons.

RODIMUS IN VEHICLE FORM

POWER SCALE

RANK	8.0	ENDURANCE	7.0
STRENGTH	8.0	COURAGE	9.0
INTELLIGENCE	8.0	FIREBLAST	8.0
SPEED	9.0	SKILL	8.0

QUOTE: "I CAN TAKE DOWN ANY DECEPTICON WITHOUT GETTING A SCRATCH."

FACT FILE

◎ Rodimus can powerlink with his Autobot brother Inferno.

POWERLINX RODIMUS

PROWL

PROFILE

Prowl is the fastest of all Omnicons, in both his robot and vehicle modes. He is also head of security for several key Autobot bases. In his vehicle mode of a Formula One police car, he has tremendous speed and maneuverability. In his robot mode, he fires a powerful cannon that unleashes Energon nets and cages capable of imprisoning any Decepticon. No enemy has ever outrun Prowl in either of his forms.

PROWL IN VEHICLE FORM

POWER SCALE

RANK	8.0	ENDURANCE	8.0
STRENGTH	7.0	COURAGE	9.0
INTELLIGENCE	8.0	FIREBLAST	7.0
SPEED	10.0	SKILL	9.0

QUOTE: "YOU CAN RUN FROM JUSTICE, BUT I'LL CATCH YOU!"

POWERLINX PROWL

FACT FILE

- Prowl can powerlink with the Inferno, Rodimus, and Hot Shot.

STRONGARM

POWER SCALE

RANK	8.0	ENDURANCE	9.0
STRENGTH	7.0	COURAGE	9.0
INTELLIGENCE	8.0	FIREBLAST	7.0
SPEED	4.0	SKILL	7.0

QUOTE: "PROVIDING FOR MY COMPANIONS GIVES ME
A PROFOUND FEELING OF ACCOMPLISHMENT."

PROFILE

Strongarm is one of the Omnicons, a special type of Autobot Transformer. Omnicons have the unique ability to harness and control Energon in its raw form. Other Autobots can't safely handle raw Energon. Strongarm and his fellow Omnicons take the raw Energon and process it into useable forms. He makes weapons, tools, and Energon chips, which give Autobots a great boost in power. Strongarm considers himself a worker, a miner, and a manufacturer, rather than a warrior, although he is sometimes forced into battle.

STRONGARM IN VEHICLE FORM

FACT FILE

- Although Strongarm would rather work than fight, when he does engage in combat, this Omnicon wields an Energon axe, which returns to his hand when thrown, like a boomerang.

- Optimus Prime greatly appreciates Strongarm's ability to create Energon chips, and considers the Omnicon a key member of his Autobot team.

SKYBLAST

POWER SCALE

RANK	5.0	ENDURANCE	8.0
STRENGTH	5.0	COURAGE	7.0
INTELLIGENCE	8.0	FIREBLAST	7.0
SPEED	7.0	SKILL	8.0

QUOTE: "MY GREATEST ALLY IS THE SKY ITSELF."

PROFILE

Although he is an Omnicon, and spends a good deal of time excavating and processing raw Energon, Skyblast enjoys combat, too. He can fly at tremendous speeds while in his vehicle form of a jet. In jet mode, Skyblast performs aerial maneuvers that his fellow Autobots consider works of art. His skill in the air is unmatched. It can often mean the difference between victory and defeat in a battle with the Decepticons. In his robot mode, Skyblast wields an impressive arsenal of Energon weapons. His most dangerous weapon is his Energon claw, which can tear through even the toughest Decepticon.

SKYBLAST IN
VEHICLE FORM

FACT FILE

- Skyblast's Energon claw, while a powerful weapon, is also very useful in excavating raw Energon. With it, he can dig through solid rock.

- Although he knows he is needed to mine Energon and fight in battles, Skyblast would much rather practice his amazing aerial stunts.

SIGNAL FLARE

PROFILE

Signal Flare is an Omnicon who is considered by his fellow Omnicons to be the greatest Energon welder of all. All of the Omnicons depend on Signal Flare's skill to complete their task of creating Energon tools and weapons. In his vehicle mode, Signal Flare can shoot a powerful Energon beam from his radar dish. This beam can then be shaped into huge tools for mining Energon or crafted into massive weapons for combat.

POWER SCALE

RANK	9.0	ENDURANCE	5.0
STRENGTH	8.0	COURAGE	8.0
INTELLIGENCE	9.0	FIREBLAST	10.0
SPEED	4.0	SKILL	9.0

QUOTE: "MY IMAGINATION IS THE KEY TO WINNING."

SIGNAL FLARE IN VEHICLE FORM

FACT FILE

⊚ Signal Flare considers himself a silent warrior. He much prefers the art of creating Energon weapons to actually using them in battle.

⊚ Although not a speedster like his fellow Omnicon Skyblast, Signal Flare's intelligence, skill, and firepower make him a highly respected Omnicon.

ARCEE

PROFILE

Arcee is an extremely fast young Omnicon. She is always ready for combat, and has proven herself to be a dedicated warrior in many battles. Her Autobot teammates are always glad to have Arcee by their side. In her vehicle mode, she is an incredibly speedy sports bike able to outrace all challengers. In her robot mode, she possesses amazing skill with her Energon bow, her favorite weapon.

ARCEE IN
VEHICLE FORM

POWER SCALE

RANK	5.0	ENDURANCE	7.0
STRENGTH	6.0	COURAGE	7.0
INTELLIGENCE	5.0	FIREBLAST	8.0
SPEED	8.0	SKILL	7.0

QUOTE: "I KNOW ONLY TWO SPEEDS...FAST
AND FASTER!"

FACT FILE

⊚ Arcee's loyalty to the Autobot is as strong as her will to fight, and as great as her tremendous speed.

⊚ Although she is young and her rank is low, Optimus Prime already considers Arcee to be one of his greatest warriors.

MEGATRON

POWER SCALE

RANK	10.0	ENDURANCE	10.0
STRENGTH	10.0	COURAGE	10.0
INTELLIGENCE	10.0	FIREBLAST	10.0
SPEED	10.0	SKILL	10.0

QUOTE: "JOIN ME AND I WILL SEND YOU TO BATTLE. DEFY ME AND I WILL SEND YOU TO OBLIVION!"

PROFILE

Megatron is still the leader of the Decepticons, but much about him has changed. During the Unicron Battles, Megatron flew into Unicron in an attempt to steal his power. He got trapped inside the planet-sized Transformer. After helping Unicron repair himself and return to full power, Megatron was reborn. Unicron totally reformatted the Decepticon leader. He may look different than he did during the Armada saga, but his goal of ruling the universe has not changed. Thanks to Unicron, Megatron now possesses a vast arsenal of weapons that make him a virtually unstoppable force. This presents an even greater challenge to the Autobots in the battle for Energon.

MEGATRON IN VEHICLE FORM

FACT FILE

- In his robot mode, Megatron uses a remote-controlled triple-change tank module to battle his enemies.

- Megatron is a gunship in his vehicle mode. He uses hyper-power wings and rotating cannons to launch devastating aerial attacks.

SCORPONOK

POWER SCALE

RANK	9.0	ENDURANCE	9.0
STRENGTH	10.0	COURAGE	9.0
INTELLIGENCE	8.0	FIREBLAST	9.0
SPEED	7.0	SKILL	10.0

QUOTE: "IF I DO NOT CRUSH YOU WITH MY CLAWS, I WILL FINISH YOU WITH MY STING!"

PROFILE

Scorponok may well be the most dangerous of all the Decepticons. Not only does he want to destroy the Autobots, but he also has his sights set on Megatron, the Decepticon leader. Scorponok hopes to assume leadership of the Decepticons before the return of Megatron. For a while, when Megatron was trapped within Unicron, the giant, planet-sized Transformer put Scorponok in charge of the Decepticons. Scorponok is corrupt, ruthless, and completely power-hungry. No matter how many battles he fights or how many worlds he conquers, Scorponok only wants more. In addition to his titanic robot mode, Scorponok has two hyper-power modes.

SCORPONOK IN VEHICLE FORM

SCORPONOK IN SCORPION FORM

FACT FILE

- In his vehicle mode, Scorponok becomes a powerful jet or a construction vehicle that's more likely to be used for destruction.

- In his hyper-power mode, Scorponok has huge mechanical claws and a deadly Energon stinger.

TIDAL WAVE

PROFILE

Tidal Wave is one of the largest of all Decepticons. In his vehicle form, he is a huge and powerful warship, and can unleash a massive assault against his enemies. Tidal Wave was exposed to a huge amount of raw Energon. This caused lots of damage and decay to various parts of his body. The injured parts of Tidal Wave have been replaced with pure refined Energon, increasing his strength and making him almost unstoppable.

POWER SCALE

RANK	4.0	ENDURANCE	5.0
STRENGTH	10.0	COURAGE	7.0
INTELLIGENCE	6.0	FIREBLAST	9.0
SPEED	4.0	SKILL	8.0

QUOTE: "IN BATTLE, THE ENEMY'S FEAR IS MY GREATEST WEAPON!"

TIDLE WAVE IN VEHICLE FORM

FACT FILE

◎ Although he is a mighty warrior, Tidal Wave's lack of intelligence holds him back from ever becoming a leader of the Decepticons.

◎ Like Demolishor, Tidal Wave worked with the Autobots. He was responsible for the defense of the Autobot city in the asteroid belt.

STARSCREAM

PROFILE

Like Megatron, Starscream has been reborn and reformatted. The extremely high dose of Energon that Unicron used to bring Starscream back to life also gave him greatly increased power. He is still learning to control the force of his own might. The hyper-power mode granted by Unicron changes this Decepticon into pure energy. This allows him to instantly transport from one location to another, moving silently, unseen, like a ghost.

STARSCREAM IN VEHICLE FORM

POWER SCALE

RANK	8.0	ENDURANCE	10.0
STRENGTH	8.0	COURAGE	7.0
INTELLIGENCE	9.0	FIREBLAST	9.0
SPEED	10.0	SKILL	10.0

QUOTE: "IT IS MY DESTINY TO LEAD!"

FACT FILE

- When Unicron reformatted him, Starscream also acquired a new power sword, making him twice as dangerous as he was before.

- Starscream still believes that he, not Megatron, should be the leader of the Decepticons.

DEMOLISHOR

PROFILE

Like his Decepticon comrades, Demolishor was given a powerful hyper-mode by Unicron that enhanced his strength and armaments. His nasty personality is matched only by his horrible weapons. Demolishor loves the thrill of battle, but what he likes best is inflicting pain on his enemies. In his new, hyper-powered vehicle mode, Demolishor is a huge dump truck equipped with mighty Energon launchers. These new high-powered weapons can take down any Autobot that goes up against Demolishor.

POWER SCALE

RANK	5.0	ENDURANCE	5.0
STRENGTH	9.0	COURAGE	5.0
INTELLIGENCE	7.0	FIREBLAST	9.0
SPEED	5.0	SKILL	7.0

QUOTE: "YOUR CRIES OF PAIN ARE MUSIC TO MY EARS!"

DEMOLISHOR IN VEHICLE FORM

FACT FILE

⊚ Like Tidal Wave, Demolishor temporarily worked with the Autobots. He was responsible for defense and security in the Autobot undersea city.

⊚ Demolishor is a re-scanned version of the Autobot missile tank.

SNOW CAT

PROFILE

Snow Cat is a reformatted version of Cyclonus. As his name implies, Snow Cat can overcome any environment or physical terrain. Steep rocky mountains? Sheer icy cliffs? Thick mud? They are no problem for Snow Cat. In his vehicle form, Snow Cat becomes an all-terrain vehicle of the toughest kind. His ability to fight anywhere under any conditions gives his Decepticon teammates a strategic advantage. Hot-headed and uncontrollable at times, Snow Cat is one of Megatron's most valuable warriors. His fierce fighting tactics are feared by his enemies, and by his Decepticon comrades!

POWER SCALE

RANK	5.0	ENDURANCE	5.0
STRENGTH	9.0	COURAGE	5.0
INTELLIGENCE	7.0	FIREBLAST	9.0
SPEED	5.0	SKILL	7.0

QUOTE: "THERE IS NO TERRAIN, OR OPPONENT, THAT I CANNOT CONQUER!"

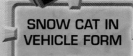

SNOW CAT IN VEHICLE FORM

FACT FILE

- Before he became hyper-powered by Unicron, Snow Cat was known as Cyclonus, a Decepticon who fought beside Megatron.

- Like Tidal Wave and Demolishor, Snow Cat once worked with the Autobots. He was responsible for guarding the Autobot city on the moon.

TERRORCONS

PROFILE

The Terrorcons are vicious, animal-like Transformers with the ability to harness and control raw Energon. They use the raw Energon to create weapons and refuel Decepticons. They were sent by Unicron to steal the Energon he needed to reformat himself. Two types of Terrorcons are the Cougar type and the Hawk type. The Hawk type flies to its target, carrying the Cougar type. When they reach a source of Energon, usually a mountain or mine, the Hawk Terrorcon shoots out a Cougar Terrorcon, who then attaches itself to the source. Using its sharp, powerful claws, the Cougar type digs out and takes the Energon. Terrorcons can clone themselves and like to run in packs like wild, predatory beasts.

There are also Terrorcons in the form of insects and dinosaurs.

FACT FILE

- When a Cougar-type Terrorcon attacks an Autobot with its razor sharp fangs, the fangs surge with Energon power and have a eerie purple glow.

- As Terrorcons extract Energon from a source, Energon storage pockets form on their backs, and glow with a purple light.

- Hawk Terrorcons fire Energon-powered feathers that strike its target like sharp throwing knives.

- Terrorcons have the ability to clone their forms to create armies of warriors.

BATTLE RAVAGE

POWER SCALE

RANK	5.0	ENDURANCE	7.0
STRENGTH	5.0	COURAGE	5.0
INTELLIGENCE	7.0	FIREBLAST	7.0
SPEED	6.0	SKILL	8.0

QUOTE: "WHAT MY CLAWS DON'T DESTROY, MY TEETH WILL!"

PROFILE

Battle Ravage is the leader of the Cougar Terrorcons. He has no emotions, and shows no mercy when attacking an enemy. Nothing stops him from reaching his goal—collecting raw Energon. In his robot mode, Battle Ravage has an assortment of incredibly powerful Energon weapons at his disposal. In his Cougar mode, he unleashes Energon-eating jaws and a devastating mace tail. Battle Ravage was created by Unicron, and he now serves his dark master, scouring the universe for Energon to steal.

BATTLE RAVAGE
IN BEAST FORM

FACT FILE

◎ Battle Ravage has an unquenchable thirst for Energon. Like a creature in the desert desperate for water, this Terrorcon is consumed by an endless hunger for the potent energy source.

◎ Battle Ravage was cloned to make the Cougar Terrorcons.

DIVEBOMB

POWER SCALE

RANK	5.0	ENDURANCE	7.0
STRENGTH	5.0	COURAGE	5.0
INTELLIGENCE	7.0	FIREBLAST	7.0
SPEED	6.0	SKILL	8.0

QUOTE: "TO CHALLENGE ME IS TO ACCEPT
YOUR DEFEAT!"

PROFILE

Divebomb is the leader of the Hawk Terrorcons. Part ninja warrior, part bird of prey, he is amazingly accurate and never misses his target. In his robot mode, his razor-sharp Energon blades and deadly slashing tools make him a very effective close-range fighter. In his Hawk mode, his Energon-enhanced feathers cut like blades and help him travel through the air with speed and precision. Swooping through the sky, he can attack from above, move in close for hand-to-hand combat, or launch a companion Cougar-type Terrorcon at an enemy or Energon source.

DIVEBOMB IN
BEAST FORM

FACT FILE

- Divebomb uses spinning leg turbines to hover in mid-air while battling his enemies in his robot mode.

- Divebomb moves silently, using ninja-like stealth to take his enemies by surprise.

CRUELLOCK

PROFILE

Of all the Terrorcons, Cruellock is the most powerful and cunning. He is not only extremely strong, but he is incredibly fast. This makes for a deadly combination. He strikes swiftly, without warning, and with great power. In his robot mode, he wields an Energon cutting blade that can slice through just about anything—or anyone. In his raptor mode, he has great leaping ability, making him almost impossible to stop during combat.

POWER SCALE

RANK	4.0	ENDURANCE	8.0
STRENGTH	8.0	COURAGE	5.0
INTELLIGENCE	8.0	FIREBLAST	6.0
SPEED	9.0	SKILL	6.0

QUOTE: "BY THE TIME YOU SEE ME
IT WILL BE TOO LATE!"

CRUELLOCK IN
RAPTOR FORM

FACT FILE

◎ Cruellock is a brilliant battle strategist with superb hunting skills.

◎ In his raptor mode, Cruellock attacks with Energon-powered claws and teeth.

INSECTICON

PROFILE

Insecticon and his clones strike like a swarm of deadly insects. He shows no mercy and has no allegiance to anyone but himself. Neither Decepticons nor Unicron fully trust him. His skill in battle is legendary, and he often leaves no survivors. Insecticon can make use of a varied arsenal of Energon-powered weapons, whether in robot mode or insect mode. He is a rare insect-type Terrorcon, and is feared by Autobots and Decepticons.

INSECTICON IN INSECT FORM

POWER SCALE

RANK	4.0	ENDURANCE	8.0
STRENGTH	9.0	COURAGE	5.0
INTELLIGENCE	4.0	FIREBLAST	8.0
SPEED	4.0	SKILL	6.0

QUOTE: "I HAVE AN APPETITE FOR YOUR DESTRUCTION!"

FACT FILE

◎ Insecticon can clone himself into a fearsome army of hundreds of attacking Terrorcons.

◎ Insecticon destroys simply for the sake of destruction, not to serve any group or cause.

PERCEPTOR

POWER SCALE

RANK	9.0	ENDURANCE	7.0
STRENGTH	7.0	COURAGE	9.0
INTELLIGENCE	8.0	FIREBLAST	6.0
SPEED	7.0	SKILL	9.0

QUOTE: "TEAMWORK IS THE KEY TO VICTORY!"

PROFILE

Perceptor is the combined robot form of three Mini-Cons: Grindor, Sureshock, and High Wire, the Street Action Mini-con Team. Although these Mini-cons were awakened by humans—Rad, Carlos, and Alexis—many years ago, the reformatted Perceptor now spends most of his time with a teenager named Kicker. Although he is a great warrior, Perceptor prefers the company of humans, and likes learning about Earth and its culture. As separate vehicles, Perceptor takes the forms of a motorbike, a four-wheel, all-terrain vehicle, and a hover-boat.

GRINDOR IN VEHICLE FORM

HIGH WIRE IN VEHICLE FORM

SURESHOCK IN VEHICLE FORM

FACT FILE

- When Grindor, Sureshock, and High Wire combine to form Perceptor, their intelligence increases dramatically.

- When Perceptor is around Kicker, he is more often in his combined form than as three separate vehicles, unlike when the Mini-cons were with Rad, Carlos, and Alexis.

43

ENERGON SABER

SCATTOR

SKYBOOM

POWER SCALE

RANK	5.0	ENDURANCE	9.0
STRENGTH	10.0	COURAGE	10.0
INTELLIGENCE	7.0	FIREBLAST	8.0
SPEED	10.0	SKILL	9.0

QUOTE: "MY GREAT POWER SHALL ONLY BE USED FOR DEFENSE AND THE PROTECTION OF THE INNOCENT."

PROFILE

The Energon Saber is formed when three Mini-cons—Wreckage, Scattor, and Skyboom—combine. The Energon Saber that results from this combination is a weapon of tremendous power. Wreckage, Scattor, and Skyboom were originally Mini-con robots made of metal. Undergoing an incredible transformation to become the Energon Saber, their metal bodies were replaced with pure raw Energon, glowing yellow like a brilliant sun. Powered by this pure raw Energon, the sword makes a devastating weapon when it is wielded on the side of justice.

WRECKAGE

THE ENERGON SABER

FACT FILE

- The Energon Saber is Kicker's main weapon. He is able to wield it as a powerful sword.

- For a time, Wreckage, Scattor, and Skyboom were trapped in pure Energon. When they emerged, they formed the Energon Saber.

ENERGON KICKER

POWER SCALE

RANK	8.0	ENDURANCE	8.0
STRENGTH	7.0	COURAGE	9.0
INTELLIGENCE	8.0	FIREBLAST	7.0
SPEED	10.0	SKILL	9.0

QUOTE: "YOU'RE TOO SLOW TO CATCH ME!"

PROFILE

Kicker is a 16-year-old human that helps the Autobots in their battle for Energon against the Decepticons. As an 8 year-old boy, Kicker was taken to live on Cybertron with his father, Dr. Jones. When Optimus Prime met Kicker, he immediately sensed that the boy had a special perception power. Optimus Prime helped Kicker to unlock this great ability, using his perception power.

Kicker can sense things before they happen. This has made him a great help to the Autobots. Kicker can be stubborn once he gets his mind set on something. He rides around on a speedy motorbike, and craves the action of battle.

KICKER IN HIS BATTLE SUIT

FACT FILE

- When Kicker puts on his battle suit, he becomes B Kicker, a powerful, robotically enhanced warrior.

- Kicker's father, Dr. Jones is the scientist who discovered that Energon could benefit both humans and Transformers.

- Kicker's mother, Miranda, and his 13-year-old sister, Sally, both live in the Autobot city on Earth.

CARLOS, RAD, ALEXIS

PROFILE

After having played such a large role in the Transformers Armada saga as children, Rad, Alexis, and Carlos have grown up. They still help the Autobots, but in different ways.

Rad, now 22, works at the Research Center on Cybertron, where parts for Transformers are built and battle suits for humans are made. Rad works with Kicker's father, Dr. Jones.

Alexis, now 21, works as a Public Information Officer for the Federal Government of Earth. She still uses her brilliant mind and computer skills to aid the Autobot cause.

Carlos, also 22, works at the Autobot city on Mars. He was there to witness the devastating Terrorcon attack, and was lucky to survive.

Rad

Alexis

Carlos